To my children, Jan and Anne,
who looked with me through the leaves
and found fish

Irmgard Lucht

Josef Guggenmos/Irmgard Lucht

Wonder-Fish from the Sea

Adapted from the German by Alvin Tresselt

Parents' Magazine Press
New York

Copyright ©1971 by Parents' Magazine Press
All rights reserved
Printed in the United States of America
Library of Congress Catalog Card Number: 78-148165
ISBN: Trade 0-8193-0482-4, Library 0-8193-0483-2

Title of original German edition: *Alle Meine Blätter*
Copyright ©1970 by Gertraud Middlehauve Verlag, Köln

Leaves, leaves,
Big leaves, little leaves.
In all the green colors of green.

Slender willow leaves that hang from weeping branches.
Big rough leaves of the hazel tree, rough like the shaggy wrappings
that hold the sweet hazelnuts. Gingko leaves, ribbed and split
like the wings of a strange green butterfly, or the tail
of an unknown fish. Dandelion leaves, jagged as the teeth
of a tawny lion from Africa. Big leaves, little leaves,
in all the green colors of green.

They burst from their tight brown winter buds. In the sunlight
they unfold, one by one, and stretch in the warm new sun.
There they stay on their twigs and branches, with only wind
and rain for companions. The wind talks to them in sighs
and whispers as it passes by, and the leaves answer
in soft rustly voices. Then the wind carries the words
from tree to tree, from leaf to leaf.

The birds come from the south to build their nests
in the friendly secret shadows of the leaves. They bustle about
as they feed their babies, safely hidden in the leafy branches.
And they chatter to one another about all the places
they have been. The wind listens and the leaves
are silent as the birds twitter and chatter together.

They tell of strange far-off places. Mexico, Yucatan,
Brazil and Tierra del Fuego which is the land of fire.
They tell of a mighty river called the Amazon
where howling monkeys go leaping through the green-lit jungle.

Only the sparrow has nothing to say. He knows every fence
and dog, and all the rusting tin cans in ditches for miles around,
but a bird that has been to the land of fire would not care
to hear about such things. And so the sparrow is quiet.

The silent leaves can only marvel at all this. All *they* know about are the leafy trees where they are. Even though the gingkos' ancestors came from China, they have been no farther than the ends of their leaf stems, not even as far as a grasshopper jumps.

But there is one part of the world the birds do not talk about.
None of the little birds in the trees can tell of the world
under the water, the world deep in the sea, the world that belongs
to the fish.
So it is that one day the wind speaks to the leaves,
and a secret message goes from tree to tree through the forest.
One by one the leaves let go of the twigs and branches.
The rough hazel leaves, slim willows and trembling aspen leaves,
the two-winged gingko leaves—even the jagged leaves of dandelions.
The wind gathers them up and carries them gently, gently
to the flowing waters of a broad river. And the leaves drift
on the water as it travels to the sea.

Then it happens.
As the leaves dip into the sea they become like fish.

The dandelion leaf is now a shimmering orange,
with a gingko leaf for a tail.
It glides through the ferny jungle at the bottom of the sea.

Two dandelion fish spawn, and the eggs find safety
among the green fronds of the water plants.

Soon the eggs hatch and the limpid waters are filled
with a hundred thousand baby fish darting about.

Leaf fish of every shape and color fill the water
with their brightness. Such fish as these have never
been seen before!

But there is someone who has been watching this magic down
under the sea. He sees the leaf fish as they swim about and he thinks,
"I will catch these fish to sell in the market. People will
be happy to buy fish such as these, for never have they seen
anything so beautiful."
And so the fisherman in his boat lowers his nets into the sea.

The leaf fish have never seen a net and they do not try
to escape. Soon the nets are filled with the wonder-fish
of the sea, and the fisherman pulls them into his boat.
But for all his trouble he finds in his nets nothing
but leaves from the forest.

Leaves, leaves,
Big leaves, little leaves,
In all the green colors of green.

It was artist IRMGARD LUCHT who conceived the idea for the book while she was experimenting with nature printing. She and her children gathered leaves and bark formations which she then dyed, printed on paper, and transformed into fish and birds. "It can even be done with a rolling pin," she says. Thus it is an art which young children might like to try themselves. Mrs. Lucht studied in Cologne and now lives with her family in Braunschweig, Germany, where she is also a kindergarten teacher.

The original German text was created by JOSEF GUGGENMOS, a popular writer of both prose and poetry for young readers in Germany. He was the winner of the German Youth Book Award in 1968.

The English adaptation is by the well-known American author, ALVIN TRESSELT, who has often written about nature in his many picture books for young children.